Shadow Chasers

To Seth and Margaret,

Thank you for leading the way, for showing me the beauty
in the shadows and that the joy is in the journey.

Books published by Running Press are available at special discounts for bulk purchases in the United States
by corporations, institutions, and other organizations. For more information, please contact the Special Markets
Department at the Perseus Books Group, 2300 Chestnut Street, Suite 200, Philadelphia, PA 19103,
or call (800) 810-4145, ext. 5000, or e-mail special.markets@perseusbooks.com.

ISBN 978-0-7624-4720-6

Library of Congress Control Number: 2013958209

9 8 7 6 5 4 3 2 1
Digit on the right indicates the number of this printing

Designed by Frances J. Soo Ping Chow
Edited by Marlo Scrimizzi
Typography: Alana Pro, Mr Moustache, and Sans Serif

Published by Running Press Kids
An Imprint of Running Press Book Publishers
A Member of the Perseus Books Group
2300 Chestnut Street
Philadelphia, PA 19103-4371

Visit us on the web!
www.runningpress.com/kids

Shadow Chasers

BY ELLY MACKAY

RP|KIDS
PHILADELPHIA · LONDON

There is a time,
as evening paints the summer sky…

when shadows come out to play.

If you follow them,

and try to catch them,
they will flit and flutter away.

Along the trees,
and through the spaces in between,

they hide beneath the leaves.

But when the wind blows,
they are on their way.

Playful shadows never stay.

Oh, the shadows, they move swiftly!

Ever changing,
just out of reach.

They race you along the garden path,

your feet as light as air,

and ... you catch one!

Only to find . . .

it isn't there.

Slippery shadows,
swimming and diving

into another world,
through the last light of day,

until they are out of sight.

And ...

Nighttime falls.

The warm house calls you.

It is time to say

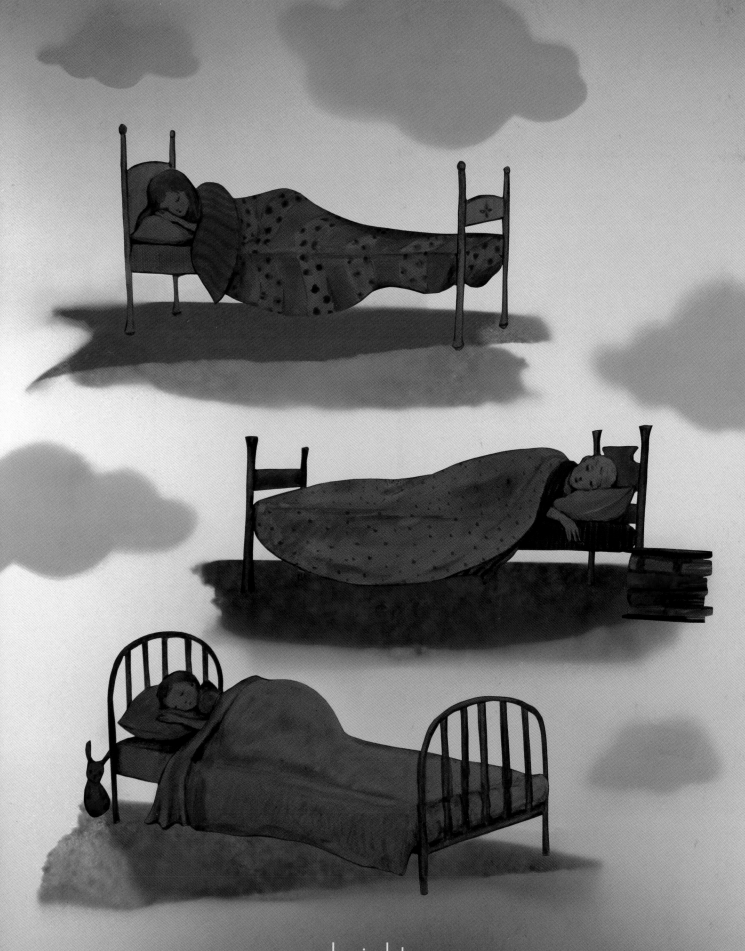

good night....

And you will meet
your shadow again,

in the early morning light.